To: Max Enjoy!

Keep your head up and
your hooves down!

Hoof wishes,

Whose Hoof is That?

Written by
Joe Garrick

Illustrations
Andrea Siles-Loayza

Design
Andres Siles-Loayza

Editing
Rachael Moyer
(Joe's Sophomore English Teacher)

Legal Consultant
Grant Sigmon

Digital Marketing Consultant & Joe's "Better Hoof"
Liz Garrick

About the Author

JOE GARRICK is the author of *Whose Hoof Is That?* and a North Carolina native. Joe grew up in Hickory, NC and attended **THE** Appalachian State University. Joe currently works in sales for a data analytics company in the healthcare industry. Joe is also an aspiring custom hat maker and the occasional wedding officiant.

Joe has always had a love for music, especially for rap and hip hop (and he even has a little musical talent himself). Though Joe's hip hop career hasn't quite taken off yet, he thought it would be nice to transition those creative skills into a different avenue that will hopefully reach a lot of people. Joe loves to make others laugh and the goal of this book is to do just that. Oh yeah, and it may also help the kids learn something.

@joe_garrick1
@whosehoofisthat

Some animals have hooves that **click**
and other animals have hooves that **clack**,
so let's learn the alphabet together
And find out

Who has hooves, feet, or wings that **flap**!

Our first friend is Arnold
An Armadillo from Austin.
He resembles the opossum
That lives up in Boston!

Arnold has four small feet
That help him dig
So he can find his food
From under the twigs.

B

Our next letter is B
So let's meet our new friend,
A big burly brown Bear
Who we all know as Ben.

Ben is from Brooklyn,
And loves everything sweet.
His favorite hobby is napping,
But Ben really loves to eat.

Ben's mom said,
"Don't play with your food
Or act like a misfit.
Now please pass the gravy
And finish your biscuit!"

Ben has four paws,
With really long nails,
And a big furry coat,
With a wiggly short tail.

We covered one and two
And now on to three,
So let's meet our new friends
And learn the letter C.

C is for Coco and Charlie,
And they are both Cows
Who like to eat grass
And moo really loud.

Coco likes to stand
Outside at the farm,
Close to where Charlie sleeps
At night in the barn.

They both have legs
That total to four
That stretch all the way down
Until they reach the floor.

There are two in the front
And two in the back,
So when Coco and Charlie run
Their hooves **click** and they **clack**!

D is for Doug,
And Doug is a Dog
Who likes to carry sticks
The size of big logs.

Doug has four legs
And each leg has a paw.
Since Doug is a good boy,
Doug comes when he's called.

Now E is for Ellie
Who has a trunk that's for smelling.
It can reach to her back
Or even tickle your belly!

TICKLE,
TICKLE?

Ellie is enormous in size,
And she is so elegant.
She has four giant feet
And never forgets
...That she is an Elephant.

F

Fast forward to F
Where we find our friend Fred,
And all day long
Fred stays in the bed.

Fred is a Fox
Who eats bagels with lox.
He is orange in color
But wears his black socks!

Hear him you won't,
But maybe you saw
The prints that he left
With his four little paws.

Gigi is from Glendale,
And she is a Giraffe.
She has a very long neck
With large spots on her back.

Gigi is tall,
And slow when she moves.
Gigi reaches real high for her food
And has four beautiful hooves.

H

Hello to you all
Some people may say "Hi!"
We have made our way to H
Where we must stop
Before we get to I.

H is our eighth letter,
And it helps to make heat.
So here is the place
Where our three H friends meet.

Harrison and Henry are Hippos,
And Harper's a Horse.
They all hail from Hawaii
And have hooves of course.

It's incredibly important
That we introduce Ilana.
She is both indigo and green,
As she's an intelligent Iguana.

With a brother named Ian
And a sister named Donna,
They travel together
And vacation in Tijuana!

Ilana likes to eat insects,
But we call them bugs.
She might run right past you
Or stop for a hug.

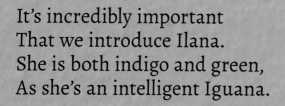

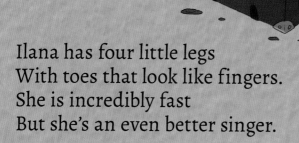

Ilana has four little legs
With toes that look like fingers.
She is incredibly fast
But she's an even better singer.

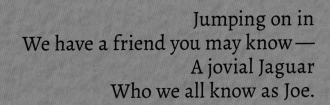

Jumping on in
We have a friend you may know—
A jovial Jaguar
Who we all know as Joe.

He has a beautiful coat
His friend Jack thinks is snazzy.
Joe may jolt from the bushes
Or even jump when he's jazzy!

Joe has very sharp claws
That are attached to four paws
Along with big shiny teeth
That rest in his jaws.

Kudos to our friend Kyle.
He's a khaki wearing dude
Who high fives with a smile
Because he's an Australian Kangaroo.

Kyle is very smart
And loves a good challenge.
He has two hands and two feet
With a big tail he uses for balance.

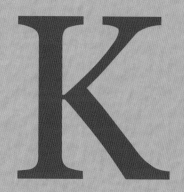

L

Let's meet our friend Lily.
She's a luxurious Llama
Who has so much personality,
And her favorite club is drama!

DRAMA,
DRAMA,
LLAMA!

Lily loves to dance
And really let loose.
She loves shaking her head
And stomping her four hooves.

TAP   TAP

Millie Millie Millie
Marching everywhere—
Millie has 750 feet,
That's 375 pairs!

With all those legs,
She could start a stampede.
And with one tough shell,
She's Millie the Millipede.

N

Nikki Nikki Nikki
Are those cans you see?
Does your narrow tusk
Help you navigate the sea?

Nikki is a Narwhal,
And we think she's pretty cute.
What makes her special
Are two rounded flippers
And a curved tail fluke.

O is for Oliver
And Oliver's an Orangutan.
Upside down by his two feet,
He loves to hang.

Along with his two feet,
Oliver has two hands.
He can open lots of doors,
Or play the oboe in the band!

P

Perhaps we press pause
And politely check the time.
Playfully waiting on us
Is Patrick the Porcupine.

With four small feet,
He prefers to stand still.
If you ask him to get to the point,
He may poke you with his quill.

We have a quick question—
Have you met our old friend?
A quail fit for a queen
Quietly known as Quinn.

She has two wings,
And the sky Quinn can paint
To match the nails on her feet,
Which we think are quite quaint.

R

We have some friends
You should get to know.
They are Ryder and Rose,
A pair of African Rhinos!

They each have four feet,
And each foot has three toes
That seem to really compliment
The horn on the tip of the nose.

Samuel is our friend
And he is a Squirrel—
The largest in fact
In the entire world!

He has four little feet
That help him climb trees
Where he hides all his nuts
So that nobody sees.

T

Top of the morning to Thomas —
The tiny Tadpole
Who will turn into a Toad
When he is ready to rock 'n' roll!

Thomas will start with a tail
That will totally disappear
As he begins to grow four legs,
So he can hop on out of here!

He may not be scared
But may seem uncertain.
Under the sea hiding
Is Uriah the Sea Urchin.

Uriah has tubed feet—
Five paired rows to be exact.
They help him stick to the floor,
So he won't float away on his back.

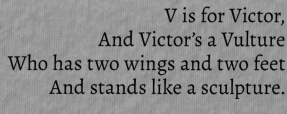

V is for Victor,
And Victor's a Vulture
Who has two wings and two feet
And stands like a sculpture.

Victor can in fact fly
As he leaves for vacation.
His distance may vary
Depending on his destination.

We know a Worm
Whose first name is Wilkes.
She loves spinning records
But prefers to spin silk!

Born with legs
That will total to ten,
One day she will wander off to sleep
And wake up as our moth friend.

X

X is for Xander,
And Xander's a Xeme.
That's an Arctic bird
You may have never seen!

Xander likes to eat bugs
And has wings he can flap.
He might dance on his two feet
When he hears eggs are the snack.

Yosef is young,
And he's also a Yak.
Who wears a big shaggy coat
From his front to his back.

If you can't see him,
He may be out having a ponder,
Where he traveled on his four hooves
To go yodel out yonder.

Z is for Zeke,
And Zeke is a Zebra.
He was born in late September
So that makes him a libra!

Zeke is pretty tired
And he needs to catch some zzzzzzz's.
He must now rest his four legs
Along with his hooves and his knees.

We made our way
From the A to the Z.
We learned the alphabet
Along with all kinds of feet.

We hope you will come back
And read with us again
At least a few more times
So you can visit with our friends!